Hoot-Hoot, Goodnight

Written by
Scott McNally

Illustrated by
Robyn McNaull

ISBN 13: 978-1-59298-859-4

Library of Congress Catalog Number: 2015946221

Printed in the United States of America

First Printing: 2016

20 19 18 17 16   5 4 3 2 1

Edited by Lily Coyle.
Cover and interior design by Laura Drew.
Digital illustration editing by Kasey Kalis.

Beaver's Pond Press
7108 Ohms Lane
Edina, MN 55439–2129
952-829-8818
www.BeaversPondBooks.com

For my Emma B

S.M.

For my own young artist and my mini adventurer

R.M.

In the evening sky
there's a magical hue,
so many colors—
orange, yellow, red, and blue.

Watch flocks of ducks and geese in flight,
gliding by, quacking and honking "goodnight."

Through the tall cattails
a glimpse of blue feather,
shows a family of mallards
all snuggled together.

This is the pond that tonight
they'll call home,
with the otters and beavers
who swim here and roam.

The sun slowly sets behind trees to the west,
as each chickadee lands in a chickadee nest.

To the east, the Man in the Moon slowly rises.
It's bedtime for critters of all shapes and sizes.

It's time to close your eyes and hear with your ears;
the soft sounds will ease away all nighttime fears.

Crickets and frogs chirp a nighty-night song.
With the full moon, they'll sing to you
all the night long.

EMMA

While you rest and dream of tomorrow's great day,
some animals are only now starting their play!
Out tiptoes the curious, sneaky raccoon,
exploring the woods by the light of the moon.

"Hoot-hoot, hoot-hoot!" comes a call in the dark,
from up in the birch tree with its white, peeling bark.
Two bright yellow eyes watch over the night,
then the owl soars away in a swift, silent flight.

And here on this night in our warm, cozy house,
all is well, all is safe, yes, even the mouse!
The cat is curled up in a kitty-cat ball
and will purr by your side until dawn's early call.

Our dog sleeps on your floor and it's hard not to giggle—
she twitches and snorts and her legs seem to jiggle.
In her dreams she's out running and exploring with you;
a big puppy lick in the morning and you'll giggle, "Eeew!"

Now it is time to close those sweet eyes.
In no time your window will hold the sunrise.
Rest and sleep sweetly, the peaceful night through,
and know, while you're dreaming, how much we love you.